THE COCOTTE

and Three Other Stories

THE COCOTTE

(Boule de Suif)

and Three Other Stories

❋

by GUY DE MAUPASSANT

Illustrated by Howard Baer

❋

FRANKLIN WATTS
London and New York

Franklin Watts Limited
18 Grosvenor Street
London W1

SBN 85166 154 8

First published in this edition 1971
© 1971 Franklin Watts Limited
Printed in Great Britain by the Westerham Press Limited

CONTENTS

In a comparatively short space of time (he was only 43 at his death) de Maupassant produced an incredible number of short stories which have enthralled readers for a century. De Maupassant was a pupil of Flaubert and his stories have the same tendency towards precision of language and rumbustious realism of situation.

In this selection we start with THE COCOTTE *(*Boule de Suif, *sometimes called "The Ball of Fat") which was in fact his earliest success (1880). Also included are "Bellflower", "Simon's Papa" and "The False Gems".*

THE COCOTTE*

FOR many days now the fag-end of the army had been straggling through the town. They were not troops, but a disbanded horde. The beards of the men were long and filthy, their uniforms in tatters, and they advanced at an easy pace without flag or regiment. All seemed worn-out and crushed, incapable of a thought or a resolution, marching by habit solely, and falling from fatigue as soon as they stopped. In short, they were a mobilized, pacific band of men, bending under the weight of the gun; some little squads on the alert, easy to take alarm and eagerly enthusiastic, ready to attack or to flee; and in the midst of them, some red breeches, the remains of a division broken up in a great battle; some sombre artillery men in line with these varied kinds of foot soldiers; and, sometimes the brilliant helmet of a dragoon on foot who followed with difficulty the shortest march of the lines.

Some legions of free-shooters, under the heroic names of "Avengers of the Defeat," "Citizens of the Tomb," "Partakers of Death," passed in their turn with the air of bandits.

Their leaders were former cloth or grain merchants, ex-merchants in tallow or soap, warriors of circumstance, elected officers on account of their escutcheons and the length of their moustaches, covered with arms and with braid, speaking in constrained voices, discussing plans of campaign, and pretending to carry agonized France alone on their swaggering shoulders, but sometimes fearing their own soldiers, prison-birds, who were often brave at first and later proved to be plunderers and debauchees.

It was said that the Prussians were going to enter Rouen.

The National Guard who for two months had been carefully reconnoitring in the neighbouring woods, shooting sometimes their own sentinels, and ready for a fight whenever a little rabbit stirred in the thicket, had now returned to their firesides. Their arms, their uniforms, all the

*Boule de Suif

murderous accoutrements with which they had lately struck fear into the national heart for three leagues in every direction, had suddenly disappeared.

The last French soldiers finally came across the Seine to reach the Audemer bridge through Saint-Sever and Bourg-Achard; and, marching behind, on foot, between two officers of ordnance, the General, in despair, unable to do anything with these incongruous remnants, himself lost in the breaking-up of a people accustomed to conquer, and disastrously beaten, in spite of his legendary bravery.

A profound calm, a frightful, silent expectancy had spread over the city. Many of the stout citizens, emasculated by commerce, anxiously awaited the conquerors, trembling lest their roasting spits or kitchen knives be considered arms.

All life seemed stopped; shops were closed, the streets dumb. Sometimes an inhabitant, intimidated by this silence, moved rapidly along beside the walls. The agony of waiting made them wish the enemy would come.

In the afternoon of the day which followed the departure of the French troops, some uhlans, coming from one knows not where, galloped through the town. Then, a little later, a black mass descended the side of St. Catharine, while two other invading bands appeared by the way of Darnetal and Boisguillaume. The advance guard of the three bodies joined one another at the same moment in Hotel de Ville square and, by all the neighbouring streets, the German army continued to arrive, spreading out its battalions, making the pavement resound under their hard, rhythmic step.

Some orders of the commander, in a foreign, guttural voice, reached the houses which seemed dead and deserted, while behind closed shutters, eyes were watching these victorious men, masters of the city, of fortunes, of lives, through the "rights of war." The inhabitants, shut up in their rooms, were visited with the kind of excitement that a cataclysm, or some fatal upheaval of the earth, brings to us, against which all force is useless. For the same sensation is produced each time that the established order of things is overturned, when security no longer exists, and all that protect the laws of man and of nature find themselves at the mercy of unreasoning, ferocious brutality. The trembling of the earth crushing the houses and burying an entire people; a river overflowing its banks and carrying in its course the drowned peasants, carcasses of beeves, and girders snatched from roofs, or a glorious army massacring those trying to defend themselves, taking others prisoners, pillaging in the name of the sword and thanking God to the sound of the cannon, all are alike frightful scourges which disconnect all belief in eternal justice, all the confidence that we have in the protection of Heaven and the reason of man.

Some detachments rapped at each door, then disappeared into the houses. It was occupation after invasion. Then it is necessary for the conquered to show themselves gracious towards the conquerors.

After some time, as soon as the first terror disappears, a new calm is established. In many families, the Prussian officer eats at the table. He is sometimes well bred and, through politeness, pities France, and speaks of his repugnance in taking part in this affair. They were grateful to him for this sentiment; then, they might be, some day or other, in need of his protection. By treating him well, they had, perhaps, a smaller number of men to feed. And why should they wound anyone on whom they were entirely dependent? To act thus would be less bravery than temerity. And temerity is no longer a fault of the commoner of Rouen, as it was at the time of the heroic defence, when their city became famous. Finally, each told himself that the highest judgment of French urbanity required that they be allowed to be polite to the strange soldier in the house, provided they did not show themselves familiar with him in public. Outside they would not make themselves known to each other, but at home they could chat freely, and the German might remain longer each evening warming his feet at their hearthstones.

The town even took on, little by little, its ordinary aspect. The French scarcely went out, but the Prussian soldiers grumbled in the streets. In short, the officers of the Blue Hussars, who dragged with arrogance their great weapons of death up and down the pavement, seemed to have no more grievous scorn for the simple citizens than the officers or the sportsmen who, the year before, drank in the same *cafés*.

There was nevertheless, something in the air, something subtle and unknown, a strange, intolerable atmosphere like a penetrating odour, the odour of invasion. It filled the dwellings and the public places, changed the taste of the food, gave the impression of being on a journey, far away, among barbarous and dangerous tribes.

The conquerors exacted money, much money. The inhabitants always paid and they were rich enough to do it. But the richer a trading Norman becomes the more he suffers at every outlay, at each part of his fortune that he sees pass from his hands into those of another.

Therefore, two or three leagues below the town, following the course of the river toward Croisset, Dieppedalle, or Biessart mariners and fishermen often picked up the swollen corpse of a German in uniform from the bottom of the river, killed by the blow of a knife, the head crushed with a stone, or perhaps thrown into the water by a push from the high bridge. The slime of the river bed buried these obscure vengeances, savage, but legitimate, unknown heroisms, mute attacks more perilous than the battles of broad day, and without the echoing sound of glory.

For hatred of the foreigner always arouses some intrepid ones, who are ready to die for an idea.

Finally, as soon as the invaders had brought the town quite under subjection with their inflexible discipline, without having been guilty of any of the horrors for which they were famous along their triumphal line of march, people began to take courage, and the need of trade put new heart into the commerce of the country. Some had large interests at Havre, which the French army occupied, and they wished to try and reach this port by going to Dieppe by land and there embarking.

They used their influence with the German soldiers with whom they had an acquaintance, and finally, an authorization of departure was obtained from the General-in-chief.

Then, a large coach, with four horses, having been engaged for this journey, ten persons engaged seats in it and resolved to set out on Tuesday morning before daylight, in order to escape observation.

For some time before, the frost had been hardening the earth and on

Monday, toward three o'clock, great black clouds coming from the north brought the snow which fell without interruption during the evening and all night.

At half past four in the morning, the travellers met in the courtyard of Hotel Normandie, where they were to take the coach.

They were still half asleep, and shivering with cold under their wraps. They could only see each other dimly in the obscure light, and the accumulation of heavy winter garments made them all resemble fat curates in long cassocks. Only two of the men were acquainted; a third accosted them and they chatted: "I'm going to take my wife," said one. "I too," said another. "And I," said the third. The first added: "We shall not return to Rouen, and if the Prussians approach Havre, we shall go over to England." All had the same intentions, being of the same mind.

As yet the horses were not harnessed. A little lantern, carried by a stable boy, went out of one door from time to time, to appear immediately at another. The feet of the horses striking the floor could be heard, although deadened by the straw and litter, and the voice of a man talking to the beasts, sometimes swearing, came from the end of the building. A light tinkling of bells announced that they were taking down the harness; this murmur soon became a clear and continuous rhythm by the movement of the animal, stopping sometimes, then breaking into a brusque shake which was accompanied by the dull stamp of a shod hoof upon the hard earth.

The door suddenly closed. All noise ceased. The frozen citizens were silent; they remained immovable and stiff.

A curtain of uninterrupted white flakes constantly sparkled in its descent to the ground. It effaced forms, and powdered everything with a downy moss. And nothing could be heard in the great silence. The town was calm, and buried under the wintry frost, as this fall of snow, undefinable and floating, a sensation rather than a sound (trembling atoms which only seem to fill all space), came to cover the earth.

The man reappeared with his lantern, pulling at the end of a rope a sad horse which would not come willingly. He placed him against the pole, fastened the traces, walked about a long time adjusting the harness, for he

had the use of but one hand, the other carrying the lantern. As he went for the second horse, he noticed the travellers, motionless, already white with snow, and said to them: "Why not get into the carriage? You will be under cover, at least."

They had evidently not thought of it, and they hastened to do so. The three men installed their wives at the back and then followed them. Then the other forms, undecided and veiled, took in their turn the last places without exchanging a word.

The floor was covered with straw, in which the feet ensconced themselves. The ladies at the back having brought little copper foot stoves, with a carbon fire, lighted them and, for some time, in low voices, enumerated the advantages of the appliances, repeating things that they had known for a long time.

Finally, the carriage was harnessed with six horses instead of four, because the travelling was very bad, and a voice called out:

"Is everybody aboard?"

And a voice within answered: "Yes."

They were off. The carriage moved slowly, slowly for a little way. The wheels were imbedded in the snow; the whole body groaned with heavy cracking sounds; the horses glistened, puffed, and smoked; and the great whip of the driver snapped without ceasing, hovering about on all sides, knotting and unrolling itself like a thin serpent, lashing brusquely some horse on the rebound, which then put forth its most violent effort.

Now the day was imperceptibly dawning. The light flakes, which one of the travellers, a Rouenese by birth, said looked like a shower of cotton wool, no longer fell. A faint light filtered through the great dull clouds, which rendered more brilliant the white of the fields, where appeared a line of great trees clothed in whiteness, or a chimney with a cap of snow.

In the carriage, each looked at the others curiously, in the sad light of this dawn.

At the end, in the best places, M. Loiseau, wholesale wine merchant, of Grand-Pont street, and Mme. Loiseau were sleeping opposite each other. Loiseau had bought out his former master who failed in business, and made his fortune. He sold bad wine at a good price to small retailers in the country, and passed among his friends and acquaintances as a knavish wag, a true Norman full of deceit and joviality.

His reputation as a sharper was so well established that one evening at the residence of the prefect, M. Tournel, author of some fables and songs, a local celebrity of keen, satirical mind, having proposed to some ladies, who seemed to be getting a little sleepy, that they make up a game of "Loiseau tricks," the joke traversed the rooms of the prefect, reached those of the town, and then, in the months to come, made many a face in the province expand with laughter.

Loiseau was especially known for his love of farce of every kind, for his jokes, good and bad; and no one could ever talk with him without thinking: "He is invaluable, this Loiseau." Of tall figure, his balloon-shaped front was surmounted by a ruddy face surrounded by grey whiskers.

His wife, large, strong, and resolute, with a quick, decisive manner, was the order and arithmetic of this house of commerce, while he was the life of it through his joyous activity.

Beside them, M. Carré-Lamadon held himself with great dignity, as if belonging to a superior caste; a considerable man, in cottons, proprietor of three mills, officer of the Legion of Honour, and member of the General Council. He had remained, during the Empire, chief of the friendly opposition, famous for making the Emperor pay more dear for rallying to the cause than if he had combated it with blunted arms, according to his own story. Mme. Carré-Lamadon, much younger than her husband, was the consolation of officers of good family sent to Rouen as the garrison. She sat opposite her husband, very dainty, petite, and pretty, wrapped closely in furs and looking with sad eyes at the interior of the carriage.

Her neighbours, the Count and Countess Hubert de Breville, bore the name of one of the most ancient and noble families of Normandy. The Count, an old gentleman of good figure, accentuated, by the artifices of his toilette, his resemblance to King Henry IV, who, according to a glorious legend of the family, had got with child one of the De Breville ladies, whose husband, for this reason, was made a count and governor of the province.

A colleague of M. Carré-Lamadon in the General Council, Count Hubert represented the Orléans party in the Department.

The story of his marriage with the daughter of an insignificant captain of a privateer had always remained a mystery. But as the Countess had a grand air, received better than anyone, and passed for having been loved by the son of Louis Philippe, all the nobility did her honour, and her salon remained the first in the country, the only one which preserved the old gallantry and to which the *entrée* was difficult. The fortune of the Brevilles amounted, it was said, to five hundred thousand francs in income, all in good securities.

These six persons formed the foundation of the carriage company, the society side, serene and strong, honest, established people, who had both religion and principles.

By a strange chance, all the women were upon the same seat; and the Countess had for neighbours two sisters who picked at long strings of beads and muttered some *Paters* and *Aves*. One was old and as pitted with small-pox as if she had received a broadside of grapeshot full in the face. The other, very sad, had a pretty face and a disease of the lungs, which, added to her devoted faith, illumined her and made her appear like a martyr.

Opposite these two devotées were a man and a woman who attracted the notice of all. The man, well known, was Cornudet the democrat, the terror of respectable people. For twenty years he had soaked his great red beard in the beer-tankards of all the democratic *cafés*. He had consumed with his friends and acquaintances a rather pretty fortune left him by his father, an old confectioner, and he awaited the establishing of the Republic with impatience, that he might have the position he merited by his great expenditures. On the fourth of September, by some joke perhaps, he believed himself elected prefect, but when he went to assume the duties, the clerks of the office were masters of the place and refused to recognize him, obliging him to retreat. Rather a fine bachelor, on the whole, inoffensive and serviceable, he had busied himself, with incomparable ardour, in organizing the defence against the Prussians. He had dug holes in all the plains, cut down young trees from the neighbouring forests, sown snares over all routes and, at the approach of the enemy, took himself quickly back to the town. He now thought he could be of more use in Havre where more entrenchments would be necessary.

The woman, one of those called a courtesan, was celebrated for her plumpness, which had given her the nick-name of "Ball-of-Fat." Small, round, and fat as lard, with puffy fingers choked at the phalanges, like chaplets of short sausages; with a stretched and shining skin, an enormous bosom which shook under her dress, she was, nevertheless, pleasing and sought after, on account of a certain freshness and breeziness of disposition. Her face was a round apple, a peony bud ready to pop into bloom, and inside that opened two great black eyes, shaded with thick brows that cast a shadow within; and below, a charming mouth, humid for kissing, furnished with shining, microscopic baby teeth. She was, it was said, full of admirable qualities.

As soon as she was recognized, a whisper went around among the honest women, and the words "prostitute" and "public shame" were whispered so loud that she raised her head. Then she threw at her neighbours such a provoking, courageous look that a great silence reigned, and everybody looked down except Loiseau, who watched her with an exhilarated air.

And immediately conversation began among the three ladies, whom the presence of this girl had suddenly rendered friendly, almost intimate. It seemed to them they should bring their married dignity into union in opposition to that sold without shame; for legal love always takes on a tone of contempt for its free *confrère*.

The three men, also drawn together by an instinct of preservation at the sight of Cornudet, talked money with a certain high tone of disdain for the poor. Count Hubert talked of the havoc which the Prussians had caused, the losses which resulted from being robbed of cattle and from destroyed crops, with the assurance of a great lord, ten times millionaire whom these ravages would scarcely cramp for a year. M. Carré-Lamadon, greatly experienced in the cotton industry, had taken care to send six hundred thousand francs to England, as a trifle in reserve if it should be needed. As for Loiseau, he had arranged with the French administration to sell them all the wines that remained in his cellars, on account of which the State owed him a formidable sum, which he counted on collecting at Havre.

And all three threw toward each other swift and amicable glances.

Although in different conditions, they felt themselves to be brothers through money, that grand free-masonry of those who possess it, and make the gold rattle by putting their hands in their trousers' pockets.

The carriage went so slowly that at ten o'clock in the morning they had not gone four leagues. The men had got down three times to climb hills on foot. They began to be disturbed because they should be now taking breakfast at Tôtes and they despaired now of reaching there before night. Each one had begun to watch for an inn along the route, when the carriage foundered in a snowdrift, and it took two hours to extricate it.

Growing appetites troubled their minds; and no eating-house, no wine shop showed itself, the approach of the Prussians and the passage of the troops having frightened away all these industries.

The gentlemen ran to the farms along the way for provisions, but they did not even find bread, for the defiant peasant had concealed his stores for fear of being pillaged by the soldiers who, having nothing to put between their teeth, took by force whatever they discovered.

Toward one o'clock in the afternoon, Loiseau announced that there was a decided hollow in his stomach. Everybody suffered with him, and the violent need of eating, ever increasing, had killed conversation.

From time to time some one yawned; another immediately imitated him; and each, in his turn, in accordance with his character, his knowledge of life, and his social position, opened his mouth with carelessness or modesty, placing his hand quickly before the yawning hole giving forth a vapour.

Ball-of-Fat, after many attempts, bent down as if seeking something under her skirts. She hesitated a second, looked at her neighbours, then sat up again quietly. Their faces were pale and drawn. Loiseau affirmed that he would give a thousand francs for a small ham. His wife made a gesture, as if in protest; but she kept quiet. She was always troubled when anyone spoke of squandering money, and could not comprehend any pleasantry on the subject. "The fact is," said the Count, "I cannot understand why I did not think to bring some provisions with me." Each reproached himself in the same way.

However, Cornudet had a flask full of rum. He offered it; it was refused coldly. Loiseau alone accepted two swallows, and then passed back the flask saying, by way of thanks: "It is good all the same; it is warming and checks the appetite." The alcohol put him in good humour and he proposed that they do as they did on the little ship in the song, eat the fattest of the passengers. This indirect allusion to Ball-of-Fat choked the well-bred people. They said nothing. Cornudet alone laughed. The two good sisters had ceased to mumble their rosaries and, with their hands enfolded in their great sleeves, held themselves immovable, obstinately lowering their eyes, without doubt offering to Heaven the suffering it had brought upon them.

Finally at three o'clock, when they found themselves in the midst of an interminable plain, without a single village in sight, Ball-of-Fat bending down quickly drew from under the seat a large basket covered with a white napkin.

At first she brought out a little china plate and a silver cup; then a large dish in which there were two whole chickens, cut up and imbedded in their own jelly. And one could still see in the basket other good things, some *pâtés*, fruits, and sweetmeats, provisions for three days if they should not see the kitchen of an inn. Four necks of bottles were seen among the packages of food. She took a wing of a chicken and began to eat it delicately, with one of those little biscuits called "Regence" in Normandy.

All looks were turned in her direction. Then the odour spread, enlarging the nostrils and making the mouth water, besides causing a painful contraction of the jaw behind the ears. The scorn of the women for this girl became ferocious, as if they had a desire to kill her and throw her out of the carriage into the snow, her, her silver cup, her basket, provisions and all.

But Loiseau with his eyes devoured the dish of chicken. He said: "Fortunately Madame had more precaution than we. There are some people who know how to think ahead always."

She turned toward him, saying: "If you would like some of it, sir? It is hard to go without breakfast so long."

He saluted her and replied: "Faith, I frankly cannot refuse; I can stand it no longer. Everything goes in time of war, does it not, Madame?" And then casting a comprehensive glance around, he added: "In moments like this, one can but be pleased to find people who are obliging."

He had a newspaper which he spread out on his knees, that no spot might come to his trousers, and upon the point of a knife that he always carried in his pocket, he took up a leg all glistening with jelly, put it between his teeth and masticated it with a satisfaction so evident that there ran through the carriage a great sigh of distress.

Then Ball-of-Fat, in a sweet and humble voice, proposed that the two sisters partake of her collation. They both accepted instantly and, without raising their eyes, began to eat very quickly, after murmuring their thanks. Cornudet no longer refused the offers of his neighbour, and they formed with the sisters a sort of table, by spreading out some newspapers upon their knees.

The mouths opened and shut without ceasing, they masticated, swallowed, gulping ferociously. Loiseau in his corner was working hard and, in a low voice, was trying to induce his wife to follow his example. She resisted for a long time; then, when a drawn sensation ran through her body, she yielded. Her husband, rounding his phrase, asked their "charming companion" if he might be allowed to offer a little piece to Madame Loiseau.

She replied: "Why, yes, certainly, sir," with an amiable smile, as she passed the dish.

An embarrassing thing confronted them when they opened the first bottle of Bordeaux: they had but one cup. Each passed it after having tasted. Cornudet alone, for politeness without doubt, placed his lips at the spot left damp by his fair neighbour.

Then, surrounded by people eating, suffocated by the odours of the food, the Count and Countess de Breville, as well as Madame and M. Carré-Lamadon, were suffering that odious torment which has preserved the name of Tantalus. Suddenly the young wife of the manufacturer gave forth such a sigh that all heads were turned in her direction; she was as white as the snow without; her eyes closed, her head drooped; she had lost consciousness. Her husband, much excited, implored the help of everybody. Each lost his head completely, until the elder of the two sisters, holding the head of the sufferer, slipped Ball-of-Fat's cup between her lips and forced her to swallow a few drops of wine. The pretty little lady revived, opened her eyes, smiled, and declared in a dying voice that she felt very well now. But, in order that the attack might not return, the sister urged her to drink a full glass of Bordeaux, and added: "It is just hunger, nothing more."

Then Ball-of-Fat, blushing and embarrassed, looked at the four travellers who had fasted and stammered: "Goodness knows! if I dared to offer anything to these gentlemen and ladies, I would—" Then she was silent, as if fearing an insult. Loiseau took up the word: "Ah! certainly, in times like these all the world are brothers and ought to aid each other. Come, ladies, without ceremony; why the devil not accept? We do not know whether we shall even find a house where we can pass the night. At the pace we are going now, we shall not reach Tôtes before noon tomorrow—"

They still hesitated, no one daring to assume the responsibility of a "Yes." The Count decided the question. He turned toward the fat, intimidated girl and, taking on a grand air of condescension, he said to her:

"We accept with gratitude, Madame."

It is the first step that counts. The Rubicon passed, they gave themselves up utterly to the occasion. The basket was stripped. It still contained a *pâté de foie gras*, a *pâté* of larks, a piece of smoked tongue, some preserved pears, a loaf of hard bread, some wafers, and a full cup of pickled gherkins and onions, of which crudities Ball-of-Fat, like all women, was extremely fond.

They could not eat this girl's provisions without speaking to her. And so they chatted, with reserve at first; then, as she carried herself well, with more abandon. The ladies de Breville and Carré-Lamadon, who were acquainted with all the ins and outs of good-breeding, were gracious with a certain delicacy. The Countess, especially, showed that amiable condescension of very noble ladies who do not fear being spoiled by contact with anyone, and was charming. But the great Mme. Loiseau, who had the soul of a plebeian, remained crabbed, saying little and eating much.

The conversation was about the war, naturally. They related the horrible deeds of the Prussians, the brave acts of the French; and all of them, although running away, did homage to those who stayed behind. Then personal stories began to be told, and Ball-of-Fat related, with sincere emotion, and in the heated words that such girls sometimes use in expressing their natural feelings, how she had left Rouen:

"I believed at first that I could remain," she said. "I had my house full of provisions, and I preferred to feed a few soldiers rather than expatriate myself, to go I knew not where. But as soon as I saw them, those Prussians, that was too much for me! They made my blood boil with anger, and I wept for very shame all day long. Oh! if I were only a man! I watched them from my windows, the great porkers with their pointed helmets, and my maid held my hands to keep me from throwing the furniture down upon them. Then one of them came to lodge at my house; I sprang at his throat the first thing; they are no more difficult to strangle than other people. And I should have put an end to that one then and there had they not pulled me away by the hair. After that, it was necessary to keep out of sight. And finally, when I found an opportunity, I left town and—here I am!"

They congratulated her. She grew in the estimation of her companions, who had not shown themselves so hot-brained, and Cornudet, while listening to her, took on the approving, benevolent smile of an apostle, as a priest would if he heard a devotée praise God, for the long-bearded democrats have a monopoly of patriotism, as the men in cassocks have of religion. In his turn he spoke, in a doctrinal tone, with the emphasis of a proclamation such as we see pasted on the walls about town, and finished by a bit of eloquence whereby he gave that "scamp of a Badinguet" a good lashing.

Then Ball-of-Fat was angry, for she was a Bonapartist. She grew redder than a cherry and, stammering with indignation, said:

"I would like to have seen you in his place, you other people. Then everything would have been quite right; oh, yes! It is you who have betrayed this man! One would never have had to leave France if it had been governed by blackguards like you!"

Cornudet, undisturbed, preserved a disdainful, superior smile, but all felt that the high note had been struck, until the Count, not without some difficulty, calmed the exasperated girl and proclaimed with a manner of authority that all sincere opinions should be respected. But the Countess and the manufacturer's wife, who had in their souls an unreasonable hatred for the people that favour a Republic, and the same instinctive tenderness that all women have for a decorative, despotic government, felt themselves drawn, in spite of themselves, toward this prostitute so full of dignity, whose sentiments so strongly resembled their own.

The basket was empty. By ten o'clock they had easily exhausted the contents and regretted that there was not more. Conversation continued for some time, but a little more coldly since they had finished eating.

The night fell, the darkness little by little became profound, and the cold, felt more during digestion, made Ball-of-Fat shiver in spite of her plumpness. Then Mme. de Breville offered her the little footstove, in which the fuel had been renewed many times since morning; she accepted it immediately, for her feet were becoming numb with cold. The ladies Carré-Lamadon and Loiseau gave theirs to the two religious sisters.

The driver had lighted his lanterns. They shone out with a lively glimmer showing a cloud of foam beyond, the sweat of the horses; and, on both sides of the way, the snow seemed to roll itself along under the moving reflection of the lights.

Inside the carriage one could distinguish nothing. But a sudden movement seemed to be made between Ball-of-Fat and Cornudet; and Loiseau, whose eye penetrated the shadow, believed that he saw the big-bearded man start back quickly as if he had received a swift, noiseless blow.

Then some twinkling points of fire appeared in the distance along the road. It was Tôtes. They had travelled eleven hours, which, with the two hours given to resting and feeding the horses, made thirteen. They entered the town and stopped before the Hotel of Commerce.

The carriage door opened! A well-known sound gave the travellers a start; it was the scabbard of a sword hitting the ground. Immediately a German voice was heard in the darkness.

Although the coach was not moving, no one offered to alight, fearing some one might be waiting to murder them as they stepped out. Then the conductor appeared, holding in his hand one of the lanterns which lighted the carriage to its depth, and showed the two rows of frightened faces, whose mouths were open and whose eyes were wide with surprise and fear.

Outside beside the driver, in full view, stood a German officer, an excessively tall young man, thin and blond, squeezed into his uniform like a girl in a corset, and wearing on his head a flat, oilcloth cap which made him resemble the porter of an English hotel. His enormous moustache, of long straight hairs, growing gradually thin at each side and terminating in a single blond thread so fine that one could not perceive where it ended, seemed to weigh heavily on the corners of his mouth and, drawing down the cheeks, left a decided wrinkle about the lips.

In Alsatian French, he invited the travellers to come in, saying in a suave tone: "Will you descend, gentlemen and ladies?"

The two good sisters were the first to obey, with the docility of saints accustomed ever to submission. The Count and Countess then appeared, followed by the manufacturer and his wife; then Loiseau, pushing ahead of him his larger half. The last-named, as he set foot on the earth, said to the officer: "Good evening, sir," more as a measure of prudence than politeness. The officer, insolent as all powerful people usually are, looked at him without a word.

Ball-of-Fat and Cornudet, although nearest the door, were the last to descend, grave and haughty before the enemy. The fat girl tried to control herself and be calm. The democrat waved a tragic hand and his long beard seemed to tremble a little and grow redder. They wished to preserve their dignity, comprehending that in such meetings as these they represented in some degree their great country, and somewhat disgusted with the docility of her companions, the fat girl tried to show more pride than her neighbours, the honest women and, as she felt that someone should set an example, she continued her attitude of resistance assumed at the beginning of the journey.

They entered the vast kitchen of the inn, and the German, having demanded their travelling papers signed by the General-in-chief (in which the name, the description, and profession of each traveller was mentioned), and having examined them all critically, comparing the people and their signatures, said: "It is quite right," and went out.

Then they breathed. They were still hungry and supper was ordered. A half hour was necessary to prepare for it, and while two servants were attending to this they went to their rooms. They found them along a corridor which terminated in a large glazed door.

Finally, they sat down at table, when the proprietor of the inn himself appeared. He was a former horse merchant, a large, asthmatic man, with a constant wheezing and rattling in his throat. His father had left him the name of Follenvie. He asked:

"Is Mlle. Elizabeth Rousset here?"

Ball-of-Fat started as she answered: "It is I."

"The Prussian officer wishes to speak with you immediately."

"With me?"

"Yes, that is, if you are Mlle. Elizabeth Rousset."

She was disturbed, and reflecting for an instant, declared flatly:

"That is my name, but I shall not go."

A stir was felt around her; each discussed and tried to think of the cause of this order. The Count approached her, saying:

"You are wrong, Madame, for your refusal may lead to considerable difficulty, not only for yourself, but for all your companions. It is never worth while to resist those in power. This request cannot assuredly bring any danger; it is, without doubt, about some forgotten formality."

Everybody agreed with him, asking, begging, beseeching her to go, and at last they convinced her that it was best; they all feared the complications that might result from disobedience. She finally said:

"It is for you that I do this, you understand."

The Countess took her by the hand, saying: "And we are grateful to you for it."

She went out. They waited before sitting down at table.

Each one regretted not having been sent for in the place of this violent, irascible girl, and mentally prepared some platitudes, in case they should be called in their turn.

But at the end of ten minutes she reappeared, out of breath, red to suffocation, and exasperated. She stammered: "Oh! the rascal; the rascal!"

All gathered around to learn something, but she said nothing; and when the Count insisted, she responded with great dignity: "No, it does not concern you; I can say nothing."

Then they all seated themselves around a tall soup tureen, whence came the odour of cabbage. In spite of alarm, the supper was gay. The cider was good, the drink Loiseau and the good sisters took as a means of economy. The others called for wine; Cornudet demanded beer. He had a special fashion of uncorking the bottle, making froth on the liquid, carefully filling the glass and then holding it before the light to appreciate the colour better. When he drank, his great beard, which still kept some of the foam of his beloved drink, seemed to tremble with tenderness; his eyes were squinted, in order not to lose sight of his tipple, and he had the unique air of fulfilling the function for which he was born. One would say that there was in his mind a meeting, like that of affinities, between the two great passions that occupied his life—Pale Ale and Revolutions; and assuredly he could not taste the one without thinking of the other.

M. and Mme. Follenvie dined at the end of the table. The man, rattling like a cracked locomotive, had too much trouble in breathing to talk while eating, but his wife was never silent. She told all her impressions at the arrival of the Prussians, what they did, what they said, reviling them because they cost her some money, and because she had two sons in the army. She addressed herself especially to the Countess, flattered by being able to talk with a lady of quality.

When she lowered her voice to say some delicate thing, her husband would interrupt, from time to time, with: "You had better keep silent,

Mme. Follenvie." But she paid no attention, continuing in this fashion:

"Yes, Madame, those people there not only eat our potatoes and pork, but our pork and potatoes. And it must not be believed that they are at all proper—oh, no! such filthy things they do, saving the respect I owe to you! And if you could see them exercise for hours in the day! they are all there in the field, marching ahead, then marching back, turning here and turning there. They might be cultivating the land, or at least working on the roads of their own country! But no, Madame, these military men are profitable to no one. Poor people have to feed them, or perhaps be murdered! I am only an old woman without education, it is true, but when I see some endangering their constitutions by raging from morning to night, I say: 'When there are so many people found to be useless, how unnecessary it is for others to take so much trouble to be nuisances! Truly, is it not an abomination to kill people, whether they be Prussian, or English, or Polish, or French? If one man revenges himself upon another who has done him some injury, it is wicked and he is punished; but when they exterminate our boys, as if they were game, with guns, they give decorations, indeed, to the one who destroys the most! Now, you see, I can never understand that, never!'"

Cornudet raised his voice: "War is a barbarity when one attacks a peaceable neighbour, but a sacred duty when one defends one's country."

The old woman lowered her head:

"Yes, when one defends himself, it is another thing; but why not make it a duty to kill all the kings who make these wars for their pleasure?"

Cornudet's eyes flashed. "Bravo, my country-woman!" said he.

M. Carré-Lamadon reflected profoundly. Although he was prejudiced as a Captain of Industry, the good sense of this peasant woman made him think of the opulence that would be brought into the country were the idle and consequently mischievous hands, and the troops which were now maintained in unproductiveness, employed in some great industrial work that it would require centuries to achieve.

Loiseau, leaving his place, went to speak with the inn-keeper in a low tone of voice. The great man laughed, shook, and squeaked, his corpulence quivered with joy at the jokes of his neighbour, and he bought of him six cases of wine for spring, after the Prussians had gone.

As soon as supper was finished, as they were worn out with fatigue, they retired.

However, Loiseau, who had observed things, after getting his wife to bed, glued his eye and then his ear to a hole in the wall, to try and discover what are known as "the mysteries of the corridor."

At the end of about an hour, he heard a groping, and, looking quickly, he perceived Ball-of-Fat, who appeared still more plump in a blue cashmere *negligée* trimmed with white lace. She had a candle in her hand and was directing her steps toward the great door at the end of the corridor. But a door at the side opened, and when she returned at the end of some minutes Cornudet, in his braces, followed her. They spoke low, then they stopped. Ball-of-Fat seemed to be defending the entrance to her room with energy. Loiseau, unfortunately, could not hear all their words, but finally, as they raised their voices, he was able to catch a few. Cornudet insisted with vivacity. He said:

"Come, now, you are a silly woman; what harm can be done?"

She had an indignant air in responding: "No, my dear, there are moments when such things are out of place. Here it would be a shame."

He doubtless did not comprehend and asked why. Then she cried out, raising her voice still more:

"Why? you do not see why? When there are Prussians in the house, in the very next room, perhaps?"

He was silent. This patriotic shame of the harlot, who would not suffer his caress so near the enemy, must have awakened the latent dignity in his heart, for after simply kissing her, he went back to his own door with a bound.

Loiseau, much excited, left the aperture, cut a caper in his room, put on his pyjamas, turned back the clothes that covered the bony frame of his companion, whom he awakened with a kiss, murmuring: "Do you love me, dearie?"

Then all the house was still. And immediately there arose somewhere,

from an uncertain quarter, which might be the cellar but was quite as likely to be the garret, a powerful snoring, monotonous and regular, a heavy, prolonged sound, like a great kettle under pressure. M. Follenvie was asleep.

As they had decided that they would set out at eight o'clock the next morning, they all collected in the kitchen. But the carriage, the roof of which was covered with snow, stood undisturbed in the courtyard, without horses and without a coachman. They sought him in vain in the stables, in the hay, and in the coach-house. Then they resolved to scour the town, and started out. They found themselves in a square, with a church at one end and some low houses on either side, where they perceived some Prussian soldiers. The first one they saw was paring potatoes. The second, further off, was cleaning the hairdresser's shop. Another, bearded to the eyes, was tending a troublesome brat, cradling it and trying to appease it; and the great peasant women, whose husbands were "away in the army," indicated by signs to their obedient conquerors the work they wished to have done: cutting wood, cooking the soup, grinding the coffee, or what not. One of them even washed the linen of his hostess, an impotent old grandmother.

The Count, astonished, asked questions of the beadle who came out of the rectory. The old man responded:

"Oh! those men are not wicked; they are not the Prussians we hear about. They are from far off, I know not where; and they have left wives and children in their country; it is not amusing to them, this war, I can tell you! I am sure they also weep for their homes, and that it makes as much sorrow among them as it does among us. Here, now, there is not so much unhappiness for the moment, because the soldiers do no harm and they work as if they were in their own homes. You see, sir, among poor people it is necessary that they aid one another. These are the great traits which war develops."

Cornudet, indignant at the cordial relations between the conquerors and the conquered, preferred to shut himself up in the inn. Loiseau had a joke for the occasion: "They will repeople the land."

M. Carré-Lamadon had a serious word: "They try to make amends."

But they did not find the driver. Finally, they discovered him in a *café* in the village, sitting at table fraternally with the officer of ordnance. The Count called out to him:

"Were you not ordered to be ready at eight o'clock?"

"Well, yes; but another order has been given me since."

"By whom?"

"Faith! the Prussian commander."

"What was it?"

"Not to harness at all."

"Why?"

"I know nothing about it. Go and ask him. They tell me not to harness, and I don't harness. That's all."

"Did he give you the order himself?"

"No, sir, the innkeeper gave the order for him."

"When was that?"

"Last evening, as I was going to bed."

The three men returned, much disturbed. They asked for M. Follenvie, but the servant answered that that gentleman, because of his asthma, never rose before ten o'clock. And he had given strict orders not to be wakened before that, except in case of fire.

They wished to see the officer, but that was absolutely impossible, since, while he lodged at the inn, M. Follenvie alone was authorized to speak to him upon civil affairs. So they waited. The women went up to their rooms again and occupied themselves with futile tasks.

Cornudet installed himself near the great chimney in the kitchen, where there was a good fire burning. He ordered one of the little tables to be brought from the *café*, then a glass of beer; he then drew out his pipe, which plays among democrats a part almost equal to his own, because in serving Cornudet it was serving its country. It was a superb pipe, an admirably coloured meerschaum, as black as the teeth of its master, but perfumed, curved, glistening, easy to the hand, completing his physiognomy. And he remained motionless, his eyes as much fixed upon the flame of the fire as upon his favourite tipple and its frothy crown; and each time that he drank, he passed his long, thin fingers through his scanty, grey hair, with an air of satisfaction, after which he sucked in his moustache fringed with foam.

Loiseau, under the pretext of stretching his legs, went to place some wine among the retailers of the country. The Count and the manufacturer began to talk politics. They could foresee the future of France. One of them believed in an Orléans, the other in some unknown saviour for the country, a hero who would reveal himself when all were in despair: a Guesclin, or a Joan of Arc, perhaps, or would it be another Napoleon the First? Ah! if the Prince Imperial were not so young!

Cornudet listened to them and smiled like one who holds the word of destiny. His pipe perfumed the kitchen.

As ten o'clock struck, M. Follenvie appeared. They asked him hurried questions; but he could only repeat two or three times without variation, these words:

"The officer said to me: 'M. Follenvie, you see to it that the carriage is not harnessed for those travellers tomorrow. I do not wish them to leave without my order. That is sufficient.'"

Then they wished to see the officer. The Count sent him his card, on which M. Carré-Lamadon wrote his name and all his titles. The Prussian sent back word that he would meet the two gentlemen after he had breakfasted, that is to say, about one o'clock.

The ladies reappeared and ate a little something, despite their disquiet. Ball-of-Fat seemed ill and prodigiously troubled.

They were finishing their coffee when the word came that the officer was ready to meet the gentlemen. Loiseau joined them; but when they tried to enlist Cornudet, to give more solemnity to their proceedings, he declared proudly that he would have nothing to do with the Germans; and he betook himself to his chimney corner and ordered another tankard of beer.

The three men mounted the staircase and were brought into the best room of the inn, where the officer received them, stretched out in an armchair, his feet on the mantel-piece, smoking a long, porcelain pipe, and enveloped in a flamboyant dressing-gown, appropriated, without doubt, from some dwelling belonging to a common citizen of bad taste. He did not

rise, nor greet them in any way, not even looking at them. It was a magnificent display of natural blackguardism transformed into the military victor.

At the expiration of some moments, he asked: "What is it you wish?"

The Count became spokesman: "We desire to go on our way, sir."

"No."

"May I ask the cause of this refusal?"

"Because I do not wish it."

"But, I would respectfully observe to you, sir, that your General-in-chief gave us permission to go to Dieppe; and I know of nothing we have done to merit your severity."

"I do not wish it—that is all; you can go."

All three having bowed, retired.

The afternoon was lamentable. They could not understand this caprice of the German; and the most singular ideas would come into their heads to trouble them. Everybody stayed in the kitchen and discussed the situation endlessly, imagining all sorts of unlikely things. Perhaps they would be retained as hostages—but to what end?—or taken prisoners—or rather a considerable ransom might be demanded. At this thought a panic prevailed. The richest were the most frightened, already seeing themselves constrained to pay for their lives with sacks of gold poured into the hands of this insolent soldier. They racked their brains to think of some acceptable falsehoods to conceal their riches and make them pass themselves off for poor people, very poor people. Loiseau took off the chain to his watch and hid it away in his pocket. The falling night increased their apprehensions. The lamp was lighted, and as there was still two hours before dinner, Madame Loiseau proposed a game of Thirty-one. It would be a diversion. They accepted. Cornudet himself, having smoked out his pipe, took part for politeness.

The Count shuffled the cards, dealt, and Ball-of-Fat had thirty-one at the outset; and immediately the interest was great enough to appease the fear that haunted their minds. Then Cornudet perceived that the house of Loiseau was given to tricks.

As they were going to the dinner table, M. Follenvie again appeared, and, in a wheezing, rattling voice, announced:

"The Prussian officer orders me to ask Mlle. Elizabeth Rousset if she has yet changed her mind."

Ball-of-Fat remained standing and was pale; then suddenly becoming crimson, such a stifling anger took possession of her that she could not speak. But finally she flashed out: "You may say to the dirty beast, that idiot, that carrion of a Prussian, that I shall never change it; you understand, never, never, never!"

The huge innkeeper went out. Then Ball-of-Fat was immediately surrounded, questioned, and solicited by all to disclose the mystery of his visit. She resisted, at first, but soon becoming exasperated, she said: "What does he want? You really want to know what he wants? He wants to sleep with me."

Everybody was choked for words, and indignation was rife. Cornudet broke his glass, so violently did he bring his fist down upon the table. There was a clamour of censure against this ignoble soldier, a blast of anger, a union of all for resistance, as if a demand had been made on each one of the party for the sacrifice exacted of her. The Count declared with disgust that those people conducted themselves after the fashion of the ancient barbarians. The women, especially, showed to Ball-of-Fat a most energetic and tender commiseration. The good sisters who only showed themselves at mealtime, lowered their heads and said nothing.

They dined, nevertheless, when the first *furore* had abated. But there was little conversation; they were thinking.

The ladies retired early, and the men, all smoking, organized a game of cards to which M. Follenvie was invited, as they intended to put a few casual questions to him on the subject of conquering the resistance of this officer. But he thought of nothing but the cards and, without listening or answering, would keep repeating: "To the game, sirs, to the game." His attention was so taken that he even forgot to spit, which must have put him some points to the good with the organ in his breast. His whistling lungs ran the whole asthmatic scale, from deep, profound tones to the sharp rustiness of a young cock essaying to crow.

He even refused to retire when his wife, who had fallen asleep previously, came to look for him. She went away alone, for she was an "early bird," always up with the sun, while her husband was a "night owl," always ready to pass the night with his friends. He cried out to her: "Leave my creamed chicken before the fire!" and then went on with his game. When they saw that they could get nothing from him, they declared that it was time to stop, and each sought his bed.

They all rose rather early the next day, with an undefined hope of getting away, which desire the terror of passing another day in that horrible inn greatly increased.

Alas! the horses remained in the stable and the driver was invisible. For want of better employment, they went out and walked around the carriage.

The breakfast was very doleful; and it became apparent that a coldness had arisen toward Ball-of-Fat, and that the night, which brings counsel, had slightly modified their judgments. They almost wished now that the Prussian had secretly found this girl, in order to give her companions a pleasant surprise in the morning. What could be more simple? Besides, who would know anything about it? She could save appearances by telling the officer that she took pity on their distress. To her, it would make so little difference!

No one had avowed these thoughts yet.

In the afternoon, as they were almost perishing from *ennui*, the Count proposed that they take a walk around the village. Each wrapped up warmly and the little party set out, with the exception of Cornudet, who preferred to remain near the fire, and the good sisters, who passed their time in the church or at the curate's.

The cold, growing more intense every day, cruelly pinched their noses and ears; their feet became so numb that each step was torture; and when they came to a field it seemed to them frightfully sad under this limitless white, so that everybody returned immediately, with hearts hard pressed and souls congealed.

The four women walked ahead, the three gentlemen followed just behind. Loiseau, who understood the situation, asked suddenly if they
thought that girl there was going to keep them long in such a place as this.
The Count, always courteous, said that they could not exact from a woman
a sacrifice so hard, unless it should come of her own will. M. Carré-
Lamadon remarked that if the French made their return through Dieppe,
as they were likely to, a battle would surely take place at Tôtes. This reflection made the two others anxious.

"If we could only get away on foot," said Loiseau.

The Count shrugged his shoulders: "How can we think of it in this
snow? and with our wives?" he said. "And then, we should be pursued and
caught in ten minutes and led back prisoners at the mercy of these soldiers."

It was true, and they were silent.

The ladies talked of their clothes, but a certain constraint seemed to
disunite them. Suddenly at the end of the street, the officer appeared. His
tall, wasp-like figure in uniform was outlined upon the horizon formed by
the snow, and he was marching with knees apart, a gait particularly military,
which is affected that they may not spot their carefully blackened boots.

He bowed in passing near the ladies and looked disdainfully at the men,
who preserved their dignity by not seeing him, except Loiseau, who made
a motion toward raising his hat.

Ball-of-Fat reddened to the ears, and the three married women resented
the great humiliation of being thus met by this soldier in the company of
this girl whom he had treated so cavalierly.

But they spoke of him, of his figure and his face. Mme. Carré-Lamadon
who had known many officers and considered herself a connoisseur of
them, found this one not at all bad; she regretted even that he was not
French, because he would make such a pretty hussar, one all the women
would rave over.

Again in the house, no one knew what to do. Some sharp words, even,
were said about things very insignificant. The dinner was silent, and
almost immediately after it, each one went to his room to kill time in sleep.

They descended the next morning with weary faces and exasperated hearts. The women scarcely spoke to Ball-of-Fat.

A bell began to ring. It was for a baptism. The fat girl had a child being brought up among the peasants of Yvetot. She had not seen it for a year, or thought of it; but now the idea of a child being baptized threw into her heart a sudden and violent tenderness for her own, and she strongly wished to be present at the ceremony.

As soon as she was gone, everybody looked at each other, then pulled their chairs together, for they thought that finally something should be decided upon. Loiseau had an inspiration: it was to hold Ball-of-Fat alone and let the others go.

M. Follenvie was charged with the commission, but he returned almost immediately, for the German, who understood human nature, had put him out. He pretended that he would retain everybody so long as his desire was not satisfied.

Then the commonplace nature of Mme. Loiseau burst out with:

"Well, we are not going to stay here to die of old age. Since it is the trade of this creature to accommodate herself to all kinds, I fail to see how she has the right to refuse one more than another. I can tell you she has received all she could find in Rouen, even the coachmen! Yes, Madame, the prefect's coachman! I know him very well, for he bought his wine at our house. And to think that today we should be drawn into this embarrassment by this affected woman, this minx! For my part, I find that this officer conducts himself very well. He has perhaps suffered privations for a long time; and doubtless he would have preferred us three; but no, he is contented with common property. He respects married women. And we must remember too that he is master. He has only to say 'I will have it,' and he could take us by force with his soldiers."

The two women had a cold shiver. Pretty Mme. Carré-Lamadon's eyes grew brilliant and she became a little pale, as if she saw herself already taken by force by the officer.

The men met and discussed the situation. Loiseau, furious, was for delivering "the wretch" bound hand and foot to the enemy. But the Count, descended from three generations of ambassadors, and endowed with the temperament of a diplomatist, was the advocate of ingenuity.

"It is best to decide upon something," said he. Then they conspired.

The women kept together, the tone of their voices was lowered, each gave advice and the discussion was general. Everything was very harmonious. The ladies especially found delicate shades and charming subtleties of expression for saying the most unusual things. A stranger would have understood nothing, so great was the precaution of language observed. But the light edge of modesty, with which every woman of the world is barbed, only covers the surface; they blossom out in a scandalous adventure of this kind, being deeply amused and feeling themselves in their element, mixing love with sensuality as a greedy cook prepares supper for his master.

Even gaiety returned, so funny did the whole story seem to them at last. The Count found some of the jokes a little off-colour, but they were so well told that he was forced to smile. In his turn, Loiseau came out with some still bolder tales, and yet nobody was wounded. The brutal thought, expressed by his wife, dominated all minds: "Since it is her trade, why should she refuse this one more than another?" The genteel Mme. Carré-Lamadon seemed to think that in her place, she would refuse this one less than some others.

They prepared the blockade at length, as if they were about to surround a fortress. Each took some rôle to play, some arguments he would bring to bear, some manoeuvres that he would endeavour to put into execution. They decided on the plan of attack, the ruse to employ, the surprise of assault, that should force this living citadel to receive the enemy in her room.

Cornudet remained apart from the rest, and was a stranger to the whole affair.

So entirely were their minds distracted that they did not hear Ball-of-Fat enter. The Count uttered a light "Ssh!" which turned all eyes in her direction. There she was. The abrupt silence and a certain embarrassment hindered them from speaking to her at first. The Countess, more accustomed to the duplicity of society than the others, finally inquired:

"Was it very amusing, that baptism?"

The fat girl, filled with emotion, told them all about it, the faces, the attitudes, and even the appearance of the church. She added: "It is good to pray sometimes."

And up to the time for luncheon these ladies continued to be amiable toward her, in order to increase her docility and her confidence in their counsel. At the table they commenced the approach. This was in the shape of a vague conversation upon devotion. They cited ancient examples: Judith and Holophernes, then, without reason, Lucrece and Sextus, and Cleopatra obliging all the generals of the enemy to pass by her couch and reducing them in servility to slaves. Then they brought out a fantastic story, hatched in the imagination of these ignorant millionaires, where the women of Rome went to Capua for the purpose of lulling Hannibal to sleep in their arms, and his lieutenants and phalanxes of mercenaries as well. They cited all the women who have been taken by conquering armies, making a battlefield of their bodies, making them also a weapon, and a means of success; and all those hideous and detestable beings who have conquered by their heroic caresses, and sacrificed their chastity to vengeance or a beloved cause. They even spoke in veiled terms of that great English family which allowed one of its women to be inoculated with a horrible and contagious disease in order to transmit it to Bonaparte, who was miraculously saved by a sudden illness at the hour of the fatal rendez-vous.

And all this was related in an agreeable, temperate fashion, except as it was enlivened by the enthusiasm deemed proper to excite emulation.

One might finally have believed that the sole duty of woman here below was a sacrifice of her person, and a continual abandonment to soldierly caprices.

The two good sisters seemed not to hear, lost as they were in profound thought. Ball-of-Fat said nothing.

During the whole afternoon they let her reflect. But, in the place of calling her "Madame" as they had up to this time, they simply called her "Mademoiselle" without knowing exactly why, as if they had a desire to put her down a degree in their esteem, which she had taken by storm, and make her feel her shameful situation.

The moment supper was served, M. Follenvie appeared with his old phrase: "The Prussian officer orders me to ask if Mlle. Elizabeth Rousset has yet changed her mind."

Ball-of-Fat responded dryly: "No, sir."

But at dinner the coalition weakened. Loiseau made three unhappy remarks. Each one beat his wits for new examples but found nothing; when the Countess, without premeditation, perhaps feeling some vague need of rendering homage to religion, asked the elder of the good sisters to tell them some great deeds in the lives of the saints. It appeared that many of their acts would have been considered crimes in our eyes; but the Church gave absolution of them readily, since they were done for the glory of God, or for the good of all. It was a powerful argument; the Countess made the most of it.

Thus it may be by one of those tacit understandings, or the veiled complacency in which anyone who wears the ecclesiastical garb excels, it may be simply from the effect of a happy unintelligence, a helpful stupidity, but in fact the religious sister lent a formidable support to the conspiracy. They had thought her timid, but she showed herself courageous, verbose, even violent. She was not troubled by the chatter of the casuist; her doctrine seemed a bar of iron; her faith never hesitated; her conscience had no scruples. She found the sacrifice of Abraham perfectly simple, for she would immediately kill father or mother on an order from on high. And nothing, in her opinion, could displease the Lord, if the intention was laudable. The Countess put to use the authority of her unwitting accomplice, and added to it the edifying paraphrase and axiom of Jesuit morals: "The need justifies the means."

Then she asked her: "Then, my sister, do you think that God accepts intentions, and pardons the deed when the motive is pure?"

"Who could doubt it, Madame? An action blamable in itself often becomes meritorious by the thought it springs from."

And they continued thus, unravelling the will of God, foreseeing his

decisions, making themselves interested in things that, in truth, they would never think of noticing. All this was guarded, skilful, discreet. But each word of the saintly sister in a cap helped to break down the resistance of the unworthy courtesan. Then the conversation changed a little, the woman of the chaplet speaking of the houses of her order, of her Superior, of herself, of her dainty neighbour, the dear sister Saint-Nicephore. They had been called to the hospitals of Havre to care for the hundreds of soldiers stricken with smallpox. They depicted these miserable creatures, giving details of the malady. And while they were stopped, *en route*, by the caprice of this Prussian officer, a great number of Frenchmen might die, whom perhaps they could have saved! It was a speciality with her, caring for soldiers. She had been in Crimea, in Italy, in Austria, and, in telling of her campaigns, she revealed herself as one of those religious aids to drums and trumpets, who seem made to follow camps, pick up the wounded in the thick of battle, and, better than an officer, subdue with a word great bands of undisciplined recruits. A true, good sister of the rataplan, whose ravaged face, marked with innumerable scars, appeared the image of the devastation of war.

No one could speak after her, so excellent seemed the effect of her words.

As soon as the repast was ended they quickly went up to their rooms, with the purpose of not coming down the next day until late in the morning.

The luncheon was quiet. They had given the grain of seed time to germinate and bear fruit. The Countess proposed that they take a walk in the afternoon. The Count, being agreeably inclined, gave an arm to Ball-of-Fat and walked behind the others with her. He talked to her in a familiar, paternal tone, a little disdainful, after the manner of men having girls in their employ, calling her "my dear child," from the height of his social position, of his undisputed honour. He reached the vital part of the question at once:

"Then you prefer to leave us here, exposed to the violences which follow a defeat, rather than consent to a favour which you have so often given in your life?"

Ball-of-Fat answered nothing.

Then he tried to reach her through gentleness, reason, and then the sentiments. He knew how to remain "The Count," even while showing himself gallant or complimentary, or very amiable if it became necessary. He exalted the service that she would render them, and spoke of her appreciation; then suddenly became gaily familiar, and said:

"And you know, my dear, it would be something for him to boast of that he had known a pretty girl; something it is difficult to find in his country."

Ball-of-Fat did not answer but joined the rest of the party. As soon as they entered the house she went to her room and did not appear again. The disquiet was extreme. What were they to do? If she continued to resist, what an embarrassment!

The dinner hour struck. They waited in vain. M. Follenvie finally entered and said that Mlle. Rousset was indisposed, and would not be at the table. Everybody pricked up his ears. The Count went to the innkeeper and said in a low voice:

"Is he in there?"

"Yes."

For convenience, he said nothing to his companions, but made a slight sign with his head. Immediately a great sigh of relief went up from every breast and a light appeared in their faces. Loiseau cried out:

"Holy Christopher! I pay for the champagne, if there is any to be found in the establishment." And Mme. Loiseau was pained to see the proprietor return with four large bottles in his hands.

Each one had suddenly become communicative and buoyant. A wanton joy filled their hearts. The Count suddenly perceived that Mme. Carré-Lamadon was charming, the manufacturer paid compliments to the Countess. The conversation was lively, gay, full of touches.

Suddenly Loiseau, with anxious face and hand upraised, called out: "Silence!" Everybody was silent, surprised, already frightened. Then he listened intently and said: "S-s-sh!" his two eyes and his hands raised toward the ceiling, listening, and then continuing, in his natural voice: "All right! All goes well!"

They failed to comprehend at first, but soon all laughed. At the end of a quarter of an hour he began the same farce again, renewing it occasionally during the whole afternoon. And he pretended to call to someone in the storey above, giving him advice in a double meaning, drawn from the fountain-head—the mind of a commercial traveller. For some moments he would assume a sad air, breathing in a whisper: "Poor girl!" Then he would murmur between his teeth, with an appearance of rage: "Ugh! That scamp of a Prussian." Sometimes, at a moment when no more was thought about it, he would say, in an affected voice, many times over: "Enough! enough!" and add, as if speaking to himself. "If we could only see her again, it isn't necessary that he should kill her, the wretch!"

Although these jokes were in deplorable taste, they amused all and wounded no one, for indignation, like other things, depends upon its surroundings, and the atmosphere which had been gradually created around them was charged with sensual thoughts.

At the dessert the women themselves made some delicate and discreet allusions. Their eyes glistened; they had drunk much. The Count, who preserved, even in his flights, his grand appearance of gravity, made a comparison, much relished, upon the subject of those wintering at the pole, and the joy of ship-wrecked sailors who saw an opening toward the south.

Loiseau suddenly arose, a glass of champagne in his hand, and said: "I drink to our deliverance." Everybody was on his feet; they shouted in agreement. Even the two good sisters consented to touch their lips to the froth of the wine which they had never before tasted. They declared that it tasted like charged lemonade, only much nicer.

Loiseau resumed: "It is unfortunate that we have no piano, for we might make up a quadrille."

Cornudet had not said a word, nor made a gesture; he appeared plunged in very grave thoughts, and made sometimes a furious motion, so that his great beard seemed to wish to free itself. Finally, toward midnight, as they were separating, Loiseau, who was staggering, touched him suddenly on the stomach and said to him in a stammer: "You are not very funny, this evening; you have said nothing, citizen!" Then Cornudet raised his head brusquely and, casting a brilliant, terrible glance around the company, said: "I tell you all that you have been guilty of infamy!" He rose, went to the door, and again repeated: "Infamy, I say!" and disappeared.

This made a coldness at first. Loiseau, disconcerted, was stupefied; but he recovered immediately and laughed heartily as he said: "He is very green, my friends. He is very green." And then, as they did not comprehend, he told them about the "mysteries of the corridor." Then there was a return of gaiety. The women behaved like lunatics. The Count and M. Carré-Lamadon wept from the force of their laughter. They could not believe it.

"How is that? Are you sure?"

"I tell you I saw it."

"And she refused—"

"Yes, because the Prussian officer was in the next room."

"Impossible!"

"I swear it!"

The Count was stifled with laughter. The industrial gentleman held his sides with both hands. Loiseau continued:

"And now you understand why he saw nothing funny this evening! No, nothing at all!" And the three started off again half ill, suffocated.

They separated. But Mme. Loiseau, who was of a spiteful nature, remarked to her husband as they were getting into bed, that "that *grisette*" of a little Carré-Lamadon was yellow with envy all the evening. "You know," she continued, "how some women will take to a uniform, whether it be French or Prussian! It is all the same to them! Oh! what a pity!"

And all night, in the darkness of the corridor, there were to be heard light noises, like whisperings and walking in bare feet, and imperceptible creakings. They did not go to sleep until late, that is sure, for there were threads of light shining under the doors for a long time. The champagne had its effect; they say it troubles sleep.

The next day a clear winter's sun made the snow very brilliant. The coach, already harnessed, waited before the door, while an army of white pigeons, in their thick plumage, with rose-coloured eyes, with a black spot in the centre, walked up and down gravely among the legs of the six horses, seeking their livelihood in the manure there scattered.

The driver, enveloped in his sheepskin, had a lighted pipe under the seat, and all the travellers, radiant, were rapidly packing some provisions for the rest of the journey. They were only waiting for Ball-of-Fat. Finally she appeared.

She seemed a little troubled, ashamed. And she advanced timidly toward her companions, who all, with one motion, turned as if they had not seen her. The Count, with dignity, took the arm of his wife and removed her from this impure contact.

The fat girl stopped, half stupefied; then, plucking up courage, she approached the manufacturer's wife with "Good morning, Madame," humbly murmured. The lady made a slight bow of the head which she accompanied with a look of outraged virtue. Everybody seemed busy, and kept themselves as far from her as if she had had some infectious disease in her skirts. Then they hurried into the carriage, where she came last, alone, and where she took the place she had occupied during the first part of the journey.

They seemed not to see her or know her; although Mme. Loiseau looking at her from afar, said to her husband in a half-tone: "Happily, I don't have to sit beside her."

The heavy carriage began to move and the remainder of the journey commenced. No one spoke at first. Ball-of-Fat dared not raise her eyes. She felt indignant toward all her neighbours, and at the same time humiliated at having yielded to the foul kisses of this Prussian, into whose arms they had hypocritically thrown her.

Then the Countess, turning toward Mme. Carré-Lamadon, broke the difficult silence:

"I believe you know Madame d'Etrelles?"

"Yes, she is one of my friends."

"What a charming woman!"

"Delightful! A very gentle nature, and well educated, besides; then she is an artist to the tips of her fingers, sings beautifully, and draws to perfection."

The manufacturer chatted with the Count, and in the midst of the rattling of the glass, an occasional word escaped such as "coupon—premium—limit—expiration."

Loiseau, who had pilfered the old pack of cards from the inn, greasy through five years of contact with tables badly cleaned, began a game of bezique with his wife.

The good sisters took from their belt the long rosary which hung there, made together the sign of the cross, and suddenly began to move their lips in a lively murmur, as if they were going through the whole of the "Oremus." And from time to time they kissed a medallion, made the sign anew, then recommenced their muttering, which was rapid and continued.

Cornudet sat motionless, thinking.

At the end of three hours on the way, Loiseau put up the cards and said: "I am hungry."

His wife drew out a package from whence she brought a piece of cold veal. She cut it evenly in thin pieces and they both began to eat.

"Suppose we do the same," said the Countess.

They consented to it and she undid the provisions prepared for the two couples. It was in one of those dishes whose lid is decorated with a china hare, to signify that a *pâté* of hare is inside, a succulent dish, where white rivers of lard cross the brown flesh of the game, mixed with some other viands hashed fine. A beautiful square of Gruyère cheese, wrapped in a piece of newspaper, preserved the imprint "divers things" upon its glutinous surface.

The two good sisters unrolled a big sausage which smelled of garlic; and Cornudet plunged his two hands into the vast pockets of his overcoat, at the same time, and drew out four hard eggs and a piece of bread. He removed the shells and threw them in the straw under his feet; then he began to eat the eggs, letting fall on his vast beard some bits of clear yellow, which looked like stars caught there.

Ball-of-Fat, in the haste and distraction of her rising, had not thought of
anything; and she looked at them exasperated, suffocating with rage, at all
of them eating so placidly. A tumultuous anger swept over her at first, and
she opened her mouth to cry out at them, to hurl at them a flood of injury
which mounted to her lips; but she could not speak, her exasperation
strangled her.

No one looked at her or thought of her. She felt herself drowned in the
scorn of these honest scoundrels, who had first sacrificed her and then
rejected her, like some improper or useless article. She thought of her great
basket full of good things which they had greedily devoured, of her two
chickens shining with jelly, of her *pâtés*, her pears, and the four bottles of
Bordeaux; and her fury suddenly falling, as a cord drawn too tightly breaks,
she felt ready to weep. She made terrible efforts to prevent it, making ugly
faces, swallowing her sobs as children do, but the tears came and glistened
in the corners of her eyes, and then two great drops, detaching themselves
from the rest, rolled slowly down like little streams of water that filter
through rock, and, falling regularly, rebounded upon her breast. She sits
erect, her eyes fixed, her face rigid and pale, hoping that no one will notice
her.

But the Countess perceives her and tells her husband by a sign. He
shrugs his shoulders, as much as to say:

"What would you have me do, it is not my fault."

Mme. Loiseau indulged in a mute laugh of triumph and murmured:

"She weeps for shame."

The two good sisters began to pray again, after having wrapped in a
paper the remainder of their sausage.

Then Cornudet, who was digesting his eggs, extended his legs to the seat
opposite, crossed them, folded his arms, smiled like a man who is watching
a good farce, and began to whistle the "Marseillaise."

All faces grew dark. The popular song assuredly did not please his
neighbours. They became nervous and agitated, having an appearance of
wishing to howl, like dogs, when they hear a barbarous organ. He perceived
this but did not stop. Sometimes he would hum the words:

> "Sacred love of country
> Help, sustain th' avenging arm;
> Liberty, sweet Liberty
> Ever fight, with no alarm."

They travelled fast, the snow being harder. But as far as Dieppe, during the long, sad hours of the journey, across the jolts in the road, through the falling night, in the profound darkness of the carriage, he continued his vengeful, monotonous whistling with a ferocious obstinacy, constraining his neighbours to follow the song from one end to the other, and to recall the words that belonged to each measure.

And Ball-of-Fat wept continually; and sometimes a sob, which she was not able to restrain, echoed between the two rows of people in the shadows.

BELLFLOWER *

How strange are those old recollections which haunt us, without our being able to get rid of them!

This one is so very old that I cannot understand how it has clung so vividly and tenaciously to my memory. Since then I have seen so many sinister things, either affecting or terrible, that I am astonished at not being able to pass a single day without the face of Mother Bellflower recurring to my mind's eye, just as I knew her formerly long, long ago, when I was ten or twelve years old.

She was an old seamstress who came to my parents' house once a week, every Thursday, to mend the linen. My parents lived in one of those country houses called châteaux, which are merely old houses with pointed roofs, to which are attached three or four adjacent farms.

The village, a large village, almost a small market town, was a few hundred yards off, and nestled round the church, a red brick church, which had become black with age.

Well, every Thursday Mother Bellflower came between half past six and seven in the morning, and went immediately into the linen-room and began to work. She was a tall, thin, bearded or rather hairy woman, for she had a beard all over her face, a surprising, an unexpected beard, growing in improbable tufts, in curly bunches which looked as if they had been sown by a madman over that great face, the face of a gendarme in petticoats. She had them on her nose, under her nose, round her nose, on her chin, on her cheeks; and her eyebrows, which were extraordinarily thick and long, and quite grey, bushy and bristling, looked exactly like a pair of moustaches stuck on there by mistake.

She limped, but not like lame people generally do, but like a ship pitching. When she planted her great, bony, vibrant body on her sound leg, she seemed to be preparing to mount some enormous wave, and then suddenly

*Clochette

she dipped as if to disappear in an abyss, and buried herself in the ground. Her walk reminded one of a ship in a storm, and her head, which was always covered with an enormous white cap, whose ribbons fluttered down her back, seemed to traverse the horizon from North to South and from South to North, at each limp.

I adored Mother Bellflower. As soon as I was up I used to go into the linen-room, where I found her installed at work, with a foot-warmer under her feet. As soon as I arrived, she made me take the foot-warmer and sit upon it, so that I might not catch cold in that large, chilly room under the roof.

"That draws the blood from your head," she would say to me.

She told me stories, while mending the linen with her long, crooked, nimble fingers; behind her magnifying spectacles, for age had impaired her sight, her eyes appeared enormous to me, strangely profound, double.

As far as I can remember from the things which she told me and by which my childish heart was moved, she had the large heart of a poor woman. She told me what had happened in the village, how a cow had escaped from the cowhouse and had been found the next morning in front of Prosper Malet's mill, looking at the sails turning, or about a hen's egg which had been found in the church belfry without anyone being able to understand what creature had been there to lay it, or the queer story of Jean Pila's dog, who had gone ten leagues to bring back his master's breeches which a tramp had stolen while they were hanging up to dry out of doors, after he had been caught in the rain. She told me these simple adventures in such a manner that in my mind they assumed the proportions of never-to-be-forgotten dramas, of grand and mysterious poems; and the ingenious stories invented by the poets, which my mother told me in the evening, had none of the flavour, none of the fullness or of the vigour of the peasant woman's narratives.

Well, one Thursday when I had spent all the morning in listening to Mother Clochette, I wanted to go upstairs to her again during the day, after picking hazelnuts with the manservant in the wood behind the farm. I remember it all as clearly as what happened only yesterday.

On opening the door of the linen-room, I saw the old seamstress lying on the floor by the side of her chair, her face turned down and her arms stretched out, but still holding her needle in one hand and one of my shirts in the other. One of her legs in a blue stocking, the longer one no doubt, was extended under her chair, and her spectacles glistened by the wall, where they had rolled away from her.

I ran away uttering shrill cries. They all came running, and in a few minutes I was told that Mother Clochette was dead.

I cannot describe the profound, poignant, terrible emotion which stirred my childish heart. I went slowly down into the drawing-room and hid myself in a dark corner, in the depths of a great, old armchair, where I knelt and wept. I remained there for a long time no doubt, for night came on. Suddenly some one came in with a lamp—without seeing me, however—and I heard my father and mother talking with the medical man, whose voice I recognized.

He had been sent for immediately, and he was explaining the cause of the accident, of which I understood nothing, however. Then he sat down and had a glass of liqueur and a biscuit.

He went on talking, and what he then said will remain engraved on my mind until I die! I think that I can give the exact words which he used.

"Ah!" said he, "the poor woman! she broke her leg the day of my arrival here. I had not even had time to wash my hands after getting off the stage-coach before I was sent for in all haste, for it was a bad case, very bad.

"She was seventeen, and a pretty girl, very pretty! Would anyone believe it? I have never told her story before, in fact no one but myself and one other person, who is no longer living in this part of the country, ever knew it. Now that she is dead, I may be less discreet.

"A young assistant teacher had just come to live in the village; he was good-looking and had the bearing of a soldier. All the girls ran after him, but he was disdainful. Besides that, he was very much afraid of his superior, the schoolmaster, old Grabu, who occasionally got out of bed the wrong foot first.

"Old Grabu already employed pretty Hortense, who has just died here, and who was afterwards nicknamed Clochette. The assistant master singled out the pretty young girl, who was no doubt flattered at being chosen by this disdainful conqueror; at any rate, she fell in love with him, and he succeeded in persuading her to give him a first meeting in the hayloft behind the school, at night after she had done her day's sewing.

"She pretended to go home, but instead of going downstairs when she left the Grabus', she went upstairs and hid among the hay, to wait for her lover. He soon joined her, and he was beginning to say pretty things to her, when the door of the hayloft opened and the schoolmaster appeared, and asked: 'What are you doing up there, Sigisbert?' Feeling sure that he would be caught, the young schoolmaster lost his presence of mind and replied stupidly: 'I came up here to rest a little among the bundles of hay, Monsieur Grabu.'

"The loft was very large and absolutely dark. Sigisbert pushed the frightened girl to the further end and said: 'Go there and hide yourself. I shall lose my situation, so get away and hide yourself.'

"When the schoolmaster heard the whispering, he continued: 'Why, you are not by yourself.'

"'Yes, I am, Monsieur Grabu!'

"'But you are not, for you are talking.'

"'I swear I am, Monsieur Grabu.'

"'I will soon find out,' the old man replied, and double-locking the door, he went down to get a light.

"Then the young man, who was a coward such as one sometimes meets, lost his head, and he repeated, having grown furious all of a sudden: 'Hide yourself, so that he may not find you. You will deprive me of my bread for my whole life; you will ruin my whole career! Do hide yourself!'

"They could hear the key turning in the lock again, and Hortense ran to the window which looked out on to the street, opened it quickly, and then in a low and determined voice said: 'You will come and pick me up when he is gone,' and she jumped out.

"Old Grabu found nobody, and went down again in great surprise. A quarter of an hour later, Monsieur Sigisbert came to me and related his adventure. The girl had remained at the foot of the wall unable to get up, as

she had fallen from the second storey, and I went with him to fetch her. It was raining in torrents, and I brought the unfortunate girl home with me, for the right leg was broken in three places, and the bones had come out through the flesh. She did not complain, and merely said, with admirable resignation: 'I am punished, well punished!'

"I sent for assistance and for the workgirl's friends and told them a made-up story of a runaway carriage which had knocked her down and lamed her, outside my door. They believed me, and the gendarmes for a whole month tried in vain to find the author of this accident.

"That is all! Now I say that this woman was a heroine, and had the fibre of those who accomplish the grandest deeds in history.

"That was her only love affair, and she died a virgin. She was a martyr, a noble soul, a sublimely devoted woman! And if I did not absolutely admire her, I should not have told you this story, which I would never tell anyone during her life: you understand why."

The doctor ceased; mamma cried and papa said some words I did not catch; then they left the room, and I remained on my knees in the armchair and sobbed, while I heard a strange noise of heavy footsteps and something knocking against the side of the staircase.

They were carrying away Clochette's body.

SIMON'S PAPA

NOON had just struck. The school-door opened and the youngsters streamed out tumbling over one another in their haste to get out quickly. But instead of promptly dispersing and going home to dinner as was their daily wont, they stopped a few paces off, broke up into knots and set to whispering.

The fact was that that morning Simon, the son of La Blanchotte, had, for the first time, attended school.

They had all of them in their families heard of La Blanchotte; and although in public she was welcome enough, the mothers among themselves treated her with compassion of a somewhat disdainful kind, which the children had caught without in the least knowing why.

As for Simon himself, they did not know him, for he never went abroad, and did not play around with them through the streets of the village or along the banks of the river. So they loved him but little; and it was with a certain delight, mingled with astonishment, that they gathered in groups this morning, repeating to each other this sentence, concocted by a lad of fourteen or fifteen who appeared to know all about it, so sagaciously did he wink: "You know Simon—well, he has no papa."

La Blanchotte's son appeared in his turn upon the threshold of the school.

He was seven or eight years old, rather pale, very neat, with a timid and almost awkward manner.

He was making his way back to his mother's house when the various groups of his schoolfellows, perpetually whispering, and watching him with the mischievous and heartless eyes of children bent upon playing a nasty trick, gradually surrounded him and ended by enclosing him altogether. There he stood amid them, surprised and embarrassed, not understanding what they were going to do with him. But the lad who had brought the news, puffed up with the success he had met with, demanded:

"What do you call yourself?"

He answered: "Simon."

"Simon what?" retorted the other.

The child, altogether bewildered, repeated: "Simon."

The lad shouted at him: "You must be named Simon something! That is not a name—Simon indeed!"

And he, on the brink of tears, replied for the third time:

"I am named Simon."

The urchins began laughing. The lad triumphantly lifted up his voice: "You can see plainly that he has no papa."

A deep silence ensued. The children were dumbfounded by this extraordinary, impossible monstrous thing—a boy who had not a papa; they looked upon him as a phenomenon, an unnatural being, and they felt rising in them the hitherto inexplicable pity of their mothers for La Blanchotte. As for Simon, he had propped himself against a tree to avoid falling, and he stood there as if paralyzed by an irreparable disaster. He sought to explain, but he could think of no answer for them, no way to deny this horrible charge that he had no papa. At last he shouted at them quite recklessly: "Yes, I have one."

"Where is he?" demanded the boy.

Simon was silent, he did not know. The children shrieked, tremendously excited. These sons of toil, nearly related to animals, experienced the cruel craving which makes the fowls of a farmyard destroy one of their own kind as soon as it is wounded. Simon suddenly spied a little neighbour, the son of a widow, whom he had always seen, as he himself was to be seen, quite alone with his mother.

"And no more have you," he said, "no more have you a papa."

"Yes," replied the other, "I have one."

"Where is he?" rejoined Simon.

"He is dead," declared the brat with superb dignity, "he is in the cemetery, is my papa."

A murmur of approval rose amid the scapegraces, as if the fact of possessing a papa dead in a cemetery made their comrade big enough to crush the

other one who had no papa at all. And these rogues, whose fathers were for the most part evil-doers, drunkards, thieves, and ill-treaters of their wives hustled each other as they pressed closer and closer to Simon as though they, the legitimate ones, would stifle in their pressure one who was beyond the law.

The lad next Simon suddenly put his tongue out at him with a waggish air and shouted at him:

"No papa! No papa!"

Simon seized him by the hair with both hands and set to work to demolish his legs with kicks, while he bit his cheek ferociously. A tremendous struggle ensued between the two boys, and Simon found himself beaten, torn, bruised, rolled on the ground in the middle of the ring of applauding little vagabonds. As he rose, mechanically brushing his little blouse all covered with dust with his hand, some one shouted at him:

"Go and tell your papa."

He then felt a great sinking in his heart. They were stronger than he, they had beaten him and he had no answer to give them, for he knew it was true that he had no papa. Full of pride he tried for some moments to struggle against the tears which were suffocating him. He had a choking fit, and then without cries he began to weep with great sobs which shook him incessantly. Then a ferocious joy broke out among his enemies, and, just like savages in fearful festivals, they took one another by the hand and danced in a circle about him as they repeated in refrain:

"No papa! No papa!"

But suddenly Simon ceased sobbing. Frenzy overtook him. There were stones under his feet; he picked them up and with all his strength hurled them at his tormentors. Two or three were struck and ran away yelling, and so formidable did he appear that the rest became panic-stricken. Cowards, like a jeering crowd in the presence of an exasperated man, they broke up and fled. Left alone, the little thing without a father set off running toward the fields, for a recollection had been awakened which nerved his soul to a great determination. He made up his mind to drown himself in the river.

He remembered, in fact, that eight days ago a poor devil who begged for

his livelihood had thrown himself into the water because he had no more
money. Simon had been there when they fished him out again; and the
sight of the fellow, who had seemed to him so miserable and ugly, had then
impressed him—his pale cheeks, his long drenched beard, and his open
eyes being full of calm. The bystanders had said:

"He is dead."

And some one had added:

"He is quite happy now."

So Simon wished to drown himself also because he had no father, just as
the wretched being did who had no money.

He reached the water and watched it flowing. Some fishes were rising
briskly in the clear stream and occasionally made little leaps and caught the
flies on the surface. He stopped crying in order to watch them, for their
feeding interested him vastly. But, at intervals, as in the lulls of a tempest,
when tremendous gusts of wind snap off trees and then die away, this
thought would return to him with intense pain:

"I am about to drown myself because I have no papa."

It was very warm and fine weather. The pleasant sunshine warmed the
grass; the water shone like a mirror; and Simon enjoyed for some minutes
the happiness of that languor which follows weeping, desirous even of falling
asleep there upon the grass in the warmth of noon.

A little green frog leaped from under his feet. He endeavoured to catch it.
It escaped him. He pursued it and lost it three times following. At last he
caught it by one of its hind legs and began to laugh as it saw the efforts the
creature made to escape. It gathered itself up on its large legs and then with
a violent spring suddenly stretched them out as stiff as two bars.

Its eyes stared wide open in their round, golden circle, and it beat the
air with its front limbs, using them as though they were hands. It reminded
him of a toy made with straight slips of wood nailed zigzag one on the other,
which by a similar movement regulated the exercise of the little soldiers
fastened thereon. Then he thought of his home and of his mother, and overcome by great sorrow he again began to weep. His lips trembled; and he
placed himself on his knees and said his prayers as before going to bed. But

he was unable to finish them, for such hurried and violent sobs overtook him that he was completely overwhelmed. He thought no more, he no longer heeded anything around him but was wholly given up to tears.

Suddenly a heavy hand was placed upon his shoulder, and a rough voice asked him:

"What is it that causes you so much grief, my fine fellow?"

Simon turned round. A tall workman, with a black beard and hair all curled, was staring at him goodnaturedly. He answered with his eyes and throat full of tears:

"They have beaten me because—I—I have no papa—no papa."

"What!" said the man smiling, "why, everybody has one."

The child answered painfully amid his spasms of grief:

"But I—I—I have none."

Then the workman became serious. He had recognized La Blanchotte's son, and although a recent arrival to the neighbourhood he had a vague idea of her history.

"Well," said he, "console yourself, my boy, and come with me home to your mother. She will give you a papa."

And so they started on the way, the big one holding the little one by the hand. The man smiled afresh, for he was not sorry to see this Blanchotte, who by popular report was one of the prettiest girls in the country-side—and, perhaps, he said to himself, at the bottom of his heart, that a lass who had erred once might very well err again.

They arrived in front of a very neat little white house.

"There it is," exclaimed the child, and he cried: "Mamma."

A woman appeared, and the workman instantly left off smiling, for he at once perceived that there was no more fooling to be done with the tall pale girl, who stood austerely at her door as though to defend from one man the threshold of that house where she had already been betrayed by another. Intimidated, his cap in his hand, he stammered out:

"See, Madame, I have brought you back your little boy, who had lost himself near the river."

But Simon flung his arms about his mother's neck and told her, as he again began to cry:

"No, mamma, I wished to drown myself, because the others had beaten me—had beaten me—because I have no papa."

A burning redness covered the young woman's cheeks, and, hurt to the quick, she embraced her child passionately, while the tears coursed down her face. The man, much moved, stood there, not knowing how to get away. But Simon suddenly ran to him and said:

"Will you be my papa?"

A deep silence ensued. La Blanchotte, dumb and tortured with shame, leaned against the wall, her hands upon her heart. The child, seeing that no answer was made him, replied:

"If you do not wish it, I shall return to drown myself."

The workman took the matter as a jest and answered laughing:

"Why, yes, I wish it certainly."

"What is your name, then," went on the child, "so that I may tell the others when they wish to know your name?"

"Philip," answered the man.

Simon was silent a moment so that he might get the name well into his memory; then he stretched out his arms, quite consoled, and said:

"Well, then, Philip, you are my papa."

The workman, lifting him from the ground, kissed him hastily on both cheeks, and then strode away quickly.

When the child returned to school next day he was received with a spiteful laugh, and at the end of school, when the lads were on the point of recommencing, Simon threw these words at their heads as he would have done a stone: "He is named Philip, my papa."

Yells of delight burst out from all sides.

"Philip who? Philip what? What on earth is Philip? Where did you pick up your Philip?"

Simon answered nothing; and immovable in faith he defied them with his eye, ready to be martyred rather than fly before them. The schoolmaster came to his rescue and he returned home to his mother.

For a space of three months, the tall workman, Philip, frequently passed by La Blanchotte's house, and sometimes made bold to speak to her when he saw her sewing near the window. She answered him civilly, always sedately, never joking with him, nor permitting him to enter her house. Notwithstanding this, being, like all men, a bit of a coxcomb, he imagined that she was often rosier than usual when she chatted with him.

But a fallen reputation is so difficult to recover, and always remains so fragile that, in spite of the shy reserve La Blanchotte maintained, they already gossiped in the neighbourhood.

As for Simon, he loved his new papa much, and walked with him nearly every evening when the day's work was done. He went regularly to school and mixed in a dignified way with his schoolfellows without ever answering them back.

One day, however, the lad who had first attacked him said to him:

"You have lied. You have not a papa named Philip."

"Why do you say that?" demanded Simon, much disturbed.

The youth rubbed his hands. He replied:

"Because if you had one he would be your mamma's husband."

Simon was confused by the truth of this reasoning; nevertheless he retorted:

"He is my papa all the same."

"That can very well be," exclaimed the urchin with a sneer, "but that is not being your papa altogether."

La Blanchotte's little one bowed his head and went off dreaming in the direction of the forge belonging to old Loizon, where Philip worked.

This forge was entombed in trees. It was very dark there, the red glare of a formidable furnace alone lit up with great flashes five blacksmiths, who hammered upon their anvils with a terrible din. Standing enveloped in flame, they worked like demons, their eyes fixed on the red-hot iron they were pounding; and their dull ideas rising and falling with their hammers.

Simon entered without being noticed and quietly plucked his friend by the sleeve. Philip turned round. All at once the work came to a standstill

and the men looked on very attentively. Then, in the midst of this un-accustomed silence, rose the little slender pipe of Simon:

"Philip, explain to me what the lad at La Michande has just told me, that you are not altogether my papa."

"And why that?" asked the smith.

The child replied in all innocence:

"Because you are not my mamma's husband."

No one laughed. Philip remained standing, leaning his forehead upon the back of his great hands, which held the handle of his hammer upright upon the anvil. He mused. His four companions watched him, and, like a tiny mite among these giants, Simon anxiously waited. Suddenly, one of the smiths, voicing the sentiment of all, said to Philip:

"All the same La Blanchotte is a good and honest girl, stalwart and steady in spite of her misfortune, and one who would make a worthy wife for an honest man."

"That is true," remarked the three others.

The smith continued:

"Is it the girl's fault if she has fallen? She had been promised marriage, and I know more than one who is much respected to-day and has sinned every bit as much."

"That is true," responded the three men in chorus.

He resumed:

"How hard she has toiled, poor thing, to educate her lad all alone, and how much she has wept since she no longer goes out, save to church, God only knows."

"That also is true," said the others.

Then no more was heard save the roar of the bellows which fanned the fire of the furnace. Philip hastily bent himself down to Simon:

"Go and tell your mamma that I shall come to speak to her."

Then he pushed the child out by the shoulders. He returned to his work and in unison the five hammers again fell upon their anvils. Thus they wrought the iron until nightfall, strong, powerful, happy, like Vulcans satisfied. But as the great bell of a cathedral resounds upon feast days above the jingling of the other bells, so Philip's hammer, dominating the noise of the others, clanged second after second with a deafening uproar. His eye on the fire, he plied his trade vigorously, erect amid the sparks.

The sky was full of stars as he knocked at La Blanchotte's door. He had his Sunday blouse on, a fresh shirt, and his beard was trimmed. The young woman showed herself upon the threshold and said in a grieved tone:

"It is ill to come thus when night has fallen, Monsieur Philip."

He wished to answer, but stammered and stood confused before her.

She resumed:

"And you understand quite well that it will not do that I should be talked about any more."

Then he said all at once:

"What does that matter to me, if you will be my wife!"

No voice replied to him, but he believed that he heard in the shadow of the room the sound of a body falling. He entered very quickly; and Simon, who had gone to his bed, distinguished the sound of a kiss and some words that his mother said very softly. Then he suddenly found himself lifted up by the hands of his friend, who, holding him at the length of his herculean arms, exclaimed to him:

"You will tell your school-fellows that your papa is Philip Remy, the blacksmith, and that he will pull the ears of all who do you any harm."

On the morrow, when the school was full and lessons about to begin, little Simon stood up quite pale with trembling lips:

"My papa," said he in a clear voice, "is Philip Remy, the blacksmith, and he has promised to box the ears of all who do me any harm."

This time no one laughed any longer, for he was very well known, was Philip Remy, the blacksmith, and he was a papa of whom anyone in the world would be proud.

THE FALSE GEMS

M. LANTIN had met the young woman at a *soirée*, at the home of the assistant chief of his bureau, and at first sight had fallen madly in love with her.

She was the daughter of a country physician who had died some months previously. She had come to live in Paris, with her mother, who visited much among her acquaintances, in the hope of making a favourable marriage for her daughter. They were poor and honest, quiet and unaffected.

The young girl was a perfect type of the virtuous woman whom every sensible young man dreams of one day winning for life. Her simple beauty had the charm of angelic modesty, and the imperceptible smile which constantly hovered about her lips seemed to be the reflection of a pure and lovely soul. Her praises resounded on every side. People were never tired of saying: "Happy the man who wins her love! He could not find a better wife."

Now M. Lantin enjoyed a snug little income, and, thinking he could safely assume the responsibilities of matrimony, proposed to this model young girl and was accepted.

He was unspeakably happy with her; she governed his household so cleverly and economically that they seemed to live in luxury. She lavished the most delicate attentions on her husband, coaxed and fondled him, and the charm of her presence was so great that six years after their marriage M. Lantin discovered that he loved his wife even more than during the first days of their honeymoon.

He only felt inclined to blame her for two things: her love of the theatre, and a taste for false jewellery. Her friends (she was acquainted with some officers' wives) frequently procured for her a box at the theatre, often for the first representations of the new plays; and her husband was obliged to accompany her, whether he willed or not, to these amusements, though they bored him excessively after a day's labour at the office.

After a time, M. Lantin begged his wife to get some lady of her acquaintance to accompany her. She was at first opposed to such an arrangement; but, after much persuasion on his part, she finally consented—to the infinite delight of her husband.

Now, with her love for the theatre came also the desire to adorn her person. True, her costumes remained as before, simple, and in the most correct taste; but she soon began to ornament her ears with huge rhinestones which glittered and sparkled like real diamonds. Around her neck she wore strings of false pearls, and on her arms bracelets of imitation gold.

Her husband frequently remonstrated with her, saying:

"My dear, as you cannot afford to buy real diamonds, you ought to appear adorned with your beauty and modesty alone, which are the rarest ornaments of your sex."

But she would smile sweetly, and say:

"What can I do? I am so fond of jewellery. It is my only weakness. We cannot change our natures."

Then she would roll the pearl necklaces around her fingers, and hold up the bright gems for her husband's admiration, gently coaxing him:

"Look! are they not lovely? One would swear they were real."

M. Lantin would then answer, smilingly:

"You have Bohemian tastes, my dear."

Often of an evening, when they were enjoying a *tête-à-tête* by the fireside, she would place on the tea table the leather box containing the "trash," as M. Lantin called it. She would examine the false gems with a passionate attention as though they were in some way connected with a deep and secret joy; and she often insisted on passing a necklace around her husband's neck, and laughing heartily would exclaim: "How droll you look!" Then she would throw herself into his arms and kiss him affectionately.

One evening in winter she attended the opera, and on her return was chilled through and through. The next morning she coughed, and eight days later died of inflammation of the lungs.

M. Lantin's despair was so great that his hair became white in one month. He wept unceasingly; his heart was torn with grief, and his mind was haunted by the remembrance, the smile, the voice—by every charm of his beautiful, dead wife.

Time, the healer, did not assuage his grief. Often during office hours, while his colleagues were discussing the topics of the day, his eyes would suddenly fill with tears, and he would give vent to his grief in heartrending sobs. Everything in his wife's room remained as before her decease; and here he was wont to seclude himself daily and think of her who had been his treasure—the joy of his existence.

But life soon became a struggle. His income, which in the hands of his wife had covered all household expenses, was now no longer sufficient for his own immediate wants; and he wondered how she could have managed to buy such excellent wines, and such rare delicacies, things which he could no longer procure with his modest resources.

He incurred some debts and was soon reduced to absolute poverty. One morning, finding himself without a sou in his pocket, he resolved to sell something, and, immediately, the thought occurred to him of disposing of his wife's paste jewels. He cherished in his heart a sort of rancour against the false gems. They had always irritated him in the past, and the very sight of them spoiled somewhat the memory of his lost darling.

To the last days of her life, she had continued to make purchases; bringing home new gems almost every evening. He decided to sell the heavy necklace which she seemed to prefer, and which, he thought, ought to be worth about six or seven francs; for although paste it was nevertheless, of very fine workmanship.

He put it in his pocket and started out in search of a jeweller's shop. He entered the first one he saw; feeling a little ashamed to expose his misery, and also to offer such a worthless article for sale.

"Sir," said he to the merchant, "I would like to know what this is worth."

The man took his necklace, examined it, called his clerk and made some remarks in an undertone; then he put the ornament back on the counter, and looked at it from a distance to judge of the effect.

M. Lantin was annoyed by all this detail and was on the point of saying: "Oh! I know well enough it is not worth anything," when the jeweller said: "Sir, that necklace is worth from twelve to fifteen thousand francs; but I could not buy it unless you tell me now whence it comes."

The widower opened his eyes wide and remained gaping, not comprehending the merchant's meaning. Finally he stammered: "You say—are you sure?" The other replied dryly: "You can search elsewhere and see if anyone will offer you more. I consider it worth fifteen thousand at the most. Come back here if you cannot do better."

M. Lantin, beside himself with astonishment, took up the necklace and left the shop. He wished time for reflection.

Once outside, he felt inclined to laugh, and said to himself: "The fool! Had I only taken him at his word! That jeweller cannot distinguish real diamonds from paste."

A few minutes after, he entered another shop in the Rue de la Paix. As soon as the proprietor glanced at the necklace, he cried out:

"Ah, *parbleu!* I know it well; it was bought here."

M. Lantin was disturbed, and asked:

"How much is it worth?"

"Well, I sold it for twenty thousand francs. I am willing to take it back for eighteen thousand when you inform me, according to our legal formality, how it comes to be in your possession."

This time M. Lantin was dumbfounded. He replied:

"But—but—examine it well. Until this moment I was under the impression that it was paste."

Said the jeweller:

"What is your name, sir?"

"Lantin—I am in the employ of the Minister of the Interior. I live at No. 16 Rue des Martyrs."

The merchant looked through his books, found the entry, and said: "That necklace was sent to Mme. Lantin's address, 16 Rue des Martyrs, July 20, 1876."

The two men looked into each other's eyes—the widower speechless

with astonishment, the jeweller scenting a thief. The latter broke the silence by saying:

"Will you leave this necklace here for twenty-four hours? I will give you a receipt."

"Certainly," answered M. Lantin, hastily. Then, putting the ticket in his pocket he left the store.

He wandered aimlessly through the streets, his mind in a state of dreadful confusion. He tried to reason, to understand. He could not afford to purchase such a costly ornament. Certainly not. But, then, it must have been a present!—a present!—a present from whom? Why was it given her?

He stopped and remained standing in the middle of the street. A horrible doubt entered his mind—she? Then all the other gems must have been presents, too! The earth seemed to tremble beneath him,—the tree before him was falling—throwing up his arms, he fell to the ground, unconscious. He recovered his senses in a pharmacy into which the passers-by had taken him, and was then taken to his home. When he arrived he shut himself up in his room and wept until nightfall. Finally, overcome with fatigue, he threw himself on the bed, where he passed an uneasy, restless night.

The following morning he arose and prepared to go to the office. It was hard to work after such a shock. He sent a letter to his employer requesting to be excused. Then he remembered that he had to return to the jeweller's. He did not like the idea; but he could not leave the necklace with that man. So he dressed and went out.

It was a lovely day; a clear blue sky smiled on the busy city below, and men of leisure were strolling about with their hands in their pockets.

Observing them, M. Lantin said to himself: "The rich, indeed, are happy. With money it is possible to forget even the deepest sorrow. One can go where one pleases, and in travel find that distraction which is the surest cure for grief. Oh! if I were only rich!"

He began to feel hungry, but his pocket was empty. He again remembered the necklace. Eighteen thousand francs! Eighteen thousand francs! What a sum!

He soon arrived in the Rue de la Paix, opposite the jeweller's. Eighteen thousand francs! Twenty times he resolved to go in, but shame kept him back. He was hungry, however,—very hungry, and had not a sou in his pocket. He decided quickly, ran across the street in order not to have time for reflection, and entered the shop.

The proprietor immediately came forward, and politely offered him a chair; the clerks glanced at him knowingly.

"I have made inquiries, M. Lantin," said the jeweller, "and if you are still resolved to dispose of the gems, I am ready to pay you the price I offered."

"Certainly, sir," stammered M. Lantin.

Whereupon the proprietor took from a drawer eighteen large bills, counted and handed them to M. Lantin, who signed a receipt and with a trembling hand put the money into his pocket.

As he was about to leave the shop, he turned toward the merchant, who still wore the same knowing smile, and lowering his eyes, said:

"I have—I have other gems which I have received from the same source. Will you buy them also?"

The merchant bowed: "Certainly, sir."

M. Lantin said gravely: "I will bring them to you." An hour later he returned with the gems.

The large diamond earrings were worth twenty thousand francs; the bracelets thirty-five thousand; the rings, sixteen thousand; a set of emeralds and sapphires, fourteen thousand; a gold chain with solitaire pendant, forty thousand—making the sum of one hundred and forty-three thousand francs.

The jeweller remarked, jokingly:

"There was a person who invested all her earnings in precious stones."

M. Lantin replied, seriously:

"It is only another way of investing one's money."

That day he lunched at Voisin's and drank wine worth twenty francs a bottle. Then he hired a carriage and made a tour of the Bois, and as he scanned the various turn-outs with a contemptuous air he could hardly refrain from crying out to the occupants:

"I, too, am rich!—I am worth two hundred thousand francs."

Suddenly he thought of his employer. He drove up to the office, and entered gaily, saying:

"Sir, I have come to resign my position. I have just inherited three hundred thousand francs."

He shook hands with his former colleagues and confided to them some of his projects for the future; then he went off to dine at the Café Anglais.

He seated himself beside a gentleman of aristocratic bearing, and during the meal informed the latter confidentially that he had just inherited a fortune of four hundred thousand francs.

For the first time in his life he was not bored at the theatre, and spent the remainder of the night in a gay frolic.

Six months afterward he married again. His second wife was a very virtuous woman, with a violent temper. She caused him much sorrow.

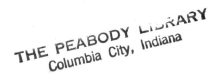